DISNEY ✦ PRINCESS

Cinderella

MOVIE CAMERA
Storybook with Film Viewer

Adapted by Judy Katschke and Olivia London
illustrated by Disney Storybook Artists

Reader's Digest
Children's Books®

Pleasantville, New York • Montréal, Québec • Bath, United Kingdom

$\mathcal{L}$ong, long ago in a tiny kingdom lived a gentle and beautiful girl named Cinderella. Cinderella lived with her cruel stepmother and mean stepsisters Drizella and Anastasia. Cinderella cooked, fed the barnyard animals, and cleaned up after everyone.

One day there was a knock at the door of Cinderella's home. It was a messenger from the palace! He had an invitation to the Prince's ball that very night!

"By royal command," he read out loud, "every eligible maiden is to attend."

Cinderella was excited—she was a maiden just like Drizella and Anastasia! But Drizella and Anastasia laughed cruelly. How could Cinderella go to the ball dressed in rags?

Her stepmother gave Cinderella permission to go to the ball, as long as she finished her chores and found a suitable dress to wear.

Drizella and Anastasia laughed out loud. How could Cinderella make a dress for the ball? And with all the chores they were about to give her, when would she ever finish?

Hopeful, Cinderella worked hard at her mountain of chores. But in her heart she knew that her only dress was too plain for the Prince's ball.

The mice and bluebirds wanted to do anything they could to help Cinderella get to the ball. So during the day, Jaq and Gus, the mice, scampered past the Stepmother's mischievous cat, Lucifer, to collect the stepsisters' discarded beads, sashes, and ribbons. They also collected scissors, needles, and thread. They had a plan to help Cinderella by making her a beautiful dress.

The animals got to work. With a stitch here and a snip there, the mice and bluebirds transformed a dress into a beautiful ball gown! The dress had originally belonged to Cinderella's mother and Cinderella's animal friends knew she would be excited to wear it.

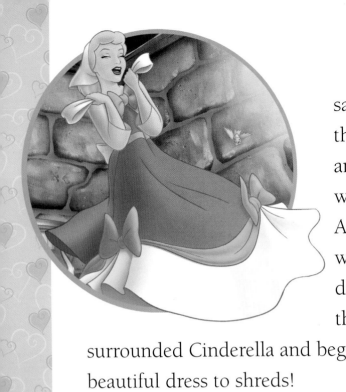

When Cinderella saw her dress she was thrilled. She tried it on and it fit perfectly. But when Drizella and Anastasia saw it they were furious. How dare Cinderella steal their things? They surrounded Cinderella and began ripping her beautiful dress to shreds!

Heartbroken, Cinderella ran out to the garden where she liked to sit under the tree and think about her mother. There she cried while her stepmother, Drizella, and Anastasia headed off to the Prince's ball. Cinderella's animal friends watched her, sad that they couldn't help.

"There's nothing left to believe in!" Cinderella sobbed.

"You don't really mean that," a gentle voice said.

Cinderella glanced up. Who said that?

A cheerful woman with twinkling eyes
smiled at Cinderella. She was Cinderella's Fairy
Godmother and she had come to help Cinderella
go to the ball!

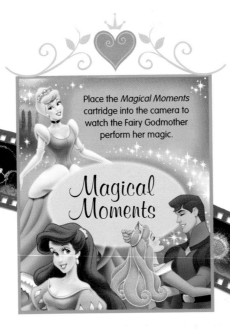

Place the *Magical Moments*
cartridge into the camera to
watch the Fairy Godmother
perform her magic.

Magical Moments

With a wave of her wand, the Fairy
Godmother turned a pumpkin into an elegant
coach. With another wave, she turned four mice
into four sturdy horses and turned a horse into
a trusty coachman!

Now Cinderella had a ride to the ball. But she
still had nothing to wear to it. Cinderella couldn't
believe her eyes. She thought, *Maybe dreams
really do come true.*

But the best was yet to come. Cinderella stood
before the Fairy Godmother in her torn dress.

With a wave of the Fairy Godmother's wand, the dress was transformed. The tattered dress became a stunning ball gown. On Cinderella's feet appeared shimmering glass slippers!

Cinderella thanked her Fairy Godmother and listened as she explained the rules: Cinderella was to leave the ball no later than the stroke of midnight—because that was when the spell would be reversed!

After waving good-bye to her friends, Cinderella climbed into her coach. Soon it was rambling its way toward the palace and the Prince's ball!

The Prince was feeling bored, when suddenly the most stunning girl appeared at the top of the staircase. The Prince did not know her name was Cinderella, he only knew she was the most beautiful girl in the kingdom!

Cinderella's stepmother watched angrily as the prince led the girl into the ballroom. Something about her was familiar, but she didn't know what it was.

Cinderella was too busy gazing into the prince's eyes to notice her wicked stepmother. As they danced, Cinderella wanted the night to last forever. But the moment she heard the clock strike midnight, she remembered her Fairy Godmother's spell!

The Prince's heart sank as Cinderella ran out of the ballroom. He still didn't know her name or where she lived. All he had left of her was the glass slipper she dropped on the staircase.

Back at her home, Cinderella watched as her coach, team of horses, and coachman turned back into what they were before. All that remained was a single glass slipper on Cinderella's foot.

All the next day Cinderella thought about the Prince and smiled. Her stepmother glared. What was the girl so happy about? But as she watched Cinderella dancing around she understood. It was Cinderella who had danced with the Prince!

Meanwhile at the palace, the King ordered the Grand Duke to find the maiden whose foot fit the lost glass slipper. By the King's command, that maiden would become the Prince's bride!

The Grand Duke went from house to house until he reached Cinderella's. Cinderella smiled when he arrived—she knew the glass slipper he carried belonged to her. But before Cinderella could try on the shoe, her stepmother locked her alone in her room!

As the palace messenger held the slipper, Drizella rammed her toes into it. Anastasia smashed her heel inside. No matter how they tried, the shoe would not fit!

Cinderella cried in her room where she sat prisoner. Her animal friends hatched a plan to free her. Jaq jumped into the Stepmother's pocket and pulled out the key to Cinderella's room. After a close call with Lucifer the cat, the mice finally unlocked the door.

Cinderella flew out of her room and down the stairs. "Your Grace?" she called. "May I try it on?"

Cinderella sat down in a chair. Then without any struggle at all the Grand Duke slipped the glass slipper on Cinderella's foot.

The Grand Duke smiled from ear to ear. He was sure that this was the girl the Prince had been looking for!

And when Cinderella rode away with the Prince in their coach she was sure of something too... that dreams really did come true!

Place the *Enchanted Moments* cartridge into the camera to watch Cinderella's wedding.

Enchanted Moments